Darcy's Dog Wash

Story by Cameron Macintosh
Illustrations by James Hart

Contents

Chapter 1

Darcy's Robots

Darcy owned a dog-grooming salon. He had a team of robots that washed, cut and brushed the dogs' hair.

"Good work, robots!" Darcy said to them one afternoon.

There had never been so many dogs in Darcy's salon.
He was very glad to see his robots giving such good service.

Just then, Darcy looked through his door
and his mouth fell open.
There was a new sign on the shop across the road:

Danzel's Dog Wash

"Oh, no!" he moaned.
"It looks like we have some competition."

Darcy was worried.
There might not be enough dogs in this town
for two robot dog-grooming salons, he thought to himself.

Chapter 2

Some Unhappy People

One afternoon, a woman came to talk to Darcy in his salon. She wasn't happy.

"Look at my poodle!" she cried.
"Can you please explain why she now has straight hair?"

A moment later, a man came over to Darcy with a bulldog and asked why it now had bright pink hair.

Then, Darcy heard a cry from a woman
on the other side of the salon.
"Why does my Dalmatian have awful green spots?"

Darcy ran out into the grooming area.

"What is going on?" he asked his robots.
But the robots just kept working
as if Darcy wasn't there.

"I'm so sorry," Darcy said to the people in the salon. "This doesn't usually happen! I'll fix these mistakes myself."

Darcy picked up his special brush and got to work. Soon, the three dogs all looked how they were meant to look.

Afterwards, Darcy spoke sternly to his robots.
"I don't want to see this happening again," he said.
"You're not programmed to make mistakes."

Darcy hoped that his robots had listened to him.

Chapter 3

A Bright Blue Labrador

The next morning, Darcy heard another angry voice in the salon.

This time, a very upset man was pointing at a Labrador. His dog had turned from a golden yellow colour to bright blue!

Darcy realised that his robots had made another big mistake. "I'm sorry," he said. "I'll fix your dog in a moment."

Just then, Darcy looked out through the door
and saw a young man on the roof of Danzel's Dog Wash.
He had a remote control in his hands and was laughing wildly.

That must be Danzel, thought Darcy.
*And it looks like he is sending remote-control radio waves
to stop my robots from working properly.*

Darcy stepped outside and looked up at Danzel. "Can you please explain what you're doing up there?" he called.

"I'm playing with my remote-controlled helicopter," said Danzel.

Darcy looked around. He couldn't see any helicopters. "I hope you're telling the truth!" he replied.

Chapter 4

Bouncing Back

When Darcy went back inside, one of his robots had started to give a small fluffy dog a *very* short haircut.

"Enough of this!" Darcy cried.

Darcy ran to the basement below his salon.
He knew there were some old robot parts down there.
A moment later, he came back
carrying a big, shiny robot arm.

Danzel was still outside on his roof,
playing with the remote control.

I'll use this robot arm to bounce the radio waves back over to Danzel's salon! Darcy thought to himself. He stood in front of his salon and lifted up the arm.

Straight away, he saw one of Danzel's robots start to shave the hair off a sheepdog.

Darcy laughed. He hoped he had taught Danzel a lesson.

Moments later, two people left Danzel's shop
with the sheepdog.
They both looked very upset
about their dog's new haircut.

Darcy felt terrible.
I think Danzel and I need to have another talk,
he said to himself.

Chapter 5

Doubling Up

Darcy went across the road
and asked Danzel for a few minutes of his time.

Straight away, Danzel said sorry
for going onto the roof to make trouble.

"I didn't have enough dogs to groom," he explained.
"I wanted to scare people away from your salon,
so they would come to mine.
I know it was wrong."

Darcy said sorry for the sheepdog's awful haircut.

"Perhaps we can find a way to do business together," said Darcy.

"I have an idea," replied Danzel. "Maybe your robots can groom small dogs, and mine can groom big dogs?"

"That sounds great!" said Darcy, cheerfully. "We'd make a good team."

The next day, they both put up the same new sign:

Darcy and Danzel's Double Dog Wash

After that, Darcy and Danzel often waved to each other
across the road, and admired the dogs
that walked out of each other's salons.

There were more than enough dogs in town for both of them!